Suddenly people were rushing toward us.

Pamela got up. "Everybody stand in a neat line. I will hand out numbers. When I call your number, you may come over and gently pat our star. Do not pluck any fur. If a stray hair sticks to your hand, you may keep it."

I stared at Pamela. She was *born* for this Hollywood thing!

First Stepping Stone Books you will enjoy:

By David A. Adler
(The Houdini Club Magic Mystery series)
Onion Sundaes
Wacky Jacks

By Kathleen Leverich
Brigid Bewitched
Brigid Beware

By Mary Pope Osborne
(The Magic Tree House series)
Pirates Past Noon (#4)
Night of the Ninjas (#5)

By Barbara Park
Junie B. Jones and Her Big Fat Mouth
Junie B. Jones and Some Sneaky Peeky Spying

By Louis Sachar
Marvin Redpost: Why Pick on Me?
Marvin Redpost: Alone in His Teacher's House

By Marjorie Weinman Sharmat
(The Genghis Khan series)
The Great Genghis Khan Look-Alike Contest (#1)
Genghis Khan: A Dog Star Is Born (#2)
Genghis Khan: Dog-Gone Hollywood (#3)

By Jerry Spinelli
Tooter Pepperday

GENGHIS KHAN:
DOG-GONE HOLLYWOOD

by Marjorie Weinman Sharmat

illustrated by Mitchell Rigie

A FIRST STEPPING STONE BOOK

Random House New York

For all the Hollywood talent scouts
who responded to my dedication in
Genghis Khan: A Dog Star Is Born,
Dudley and I are sifting through your offers
and will get back to you and do lunch.

—M. W. S.

To Nancy, my muse of happiness, joy, and
laughter. —M. R.

Text copyright © 1995 by Marjorie Weinman Sharmat
Illustrations copyright © 1995 by Mitchell Rigie
All rights reserved under International and Pan-American
Copyright Conventions. Published in the United States by
Random House, Inc., New York, and simultaneously in Canada
by Random House of Canada Limited, Toronto.

Library of Congress Cataloging-in-Publication Data
Sharmat, Marjorie Weinman.
Genghis Khan: dog-gone Hollywood / by Marjorie Weinman Sharmat ;
illustrated by Mitchell Rigie.
    p. cm. "A First stepping stone book."
Sequel to: Genghis Khan, a dog star is born.
SUMMARY: Now a major movie star, Genghis Khan, also known as Duz,
finds himself in serious competition for the Oscar in the category
of best male actor.
ISBN 0-679-86953-0 (pbk.) — ISBN 0-679-96953-5 (lib. bdg.)
[1. Dogs—Fiction.   2. Motion pictures—Production and direction—
Fiction.   3. Academy Awards (Motion pictures)—Fiction.]
I. Rigie, Mitchell, ill.   II. Title.
PZ7.S5299Gbh 1995   [Fic]—dc20   94-36081

Manufactured in the United States of America 10 9 8 7 6 5 4 3 2 1

GENGHIS KHAN:
DOG-GONE HOLLYWOOD

I love my dog. He's ugly-looking and famous. He's famous because he's ugly-looking.

His real name is Duz. But to the world, he's Genghis Khan, major movie dog star.

Duz used to be just a dog. He was a stray when I found him. I entered him in a contest. He had to look ugly enough to become the next Genghis Khan.

He won and became a star.

Now we have this big house with a swimming pool. Thanks to Duz.

Duz worked very hard on his first movie. It's called *Genghis Khan: The Challenge*. In it Duz is up against the scariest creature ever seen on a movie screen. The SLIME-OOOOOZY!

The movie is now playing all over the country.

But Duz became a *tired* star. A pooped pooch. It was time for Duz to rest. And do some fun things.

I was dipping my toes in our pool when my father said, "Let's do something special for Duz. Let's take him to the fanciest restaurant in town."

"Yes, the fanciest!" Pamela said.

Pamela Brinkman is my best friend. I knew her before I moved to Hollywood. Now she's moved to Hollywood, too.

Pamela really *is* a friend. She's seen

Duz's movie eleven times so far. I've only seen it nine times.

My mother said, "We've never been to La Roillangelique. I hear it's a terrific restaurant."

"What's Duz going to wear?" Pamela asked.

"Just his fur," I said. "He's a dog."

Pamela groaned. "Fred Shedd, thanks for the news. But what you have here is a movie-star dog. So, shouldn't he wear his Genghis Khan costume?"

"No, let him be regular Duz," I said.

"Let Duz decide," my father said.

I patted Duz.

"Bark once for Duz and twice for Genghis," I said.

Duz licked me.

Pamela sighed. "What does *that* mean?"

"It means he's hungry," I said.

"Okay," Pamela said. "No clothes for Duz."

"Except for a collar," I said. "All dogs need that."

"I'll call Fritz and have him bring the limo around," my father said.

"No," I said. "Let's drive ourselves. Tonight let's just be plain folks. Two grownups, two kids, and one dog."

My mother smiled. "Fine. I predict a perfect evening."

My mother should never become a fortune-teller.

A perfect evening was not in our future. Maybe perfectly awful...

We drove to La Roillangelique. I can't pronounce it. I can't spell it. And I don't know what it means. But they have food there.

The restaurant was all lit up on the outside. Sparkling lights. Neon signs. Even neon palm trees.

One after another, shiny long limos were pulling up to the door.

We parked our car around the corner.

We walked inside.

But not very far.

"Stop!" a man said.

He was standing near the door. He was all dressed up. In a dark suit, dark shiny shoes, and dark shiny hair.

Everything about him matched.

I hate that.

"You can't bring a dog into this restaurant," he said.

Pamela got angry. "This isn't a dog," she said. "I mean..."

"Young lady, he looks like a dog to me," the man said. "He has four feet, a tail, fur, fangs...."

Suddenly the man stepped backward. "Does he bite?"

"No," I said. "But everybody asks that. That's why his name is Duz. It's short for 'Does he bite.' He looks scary, but he's sweet."

Pamela tugged at the man's sleeve.

"Do you allow movie stars in your restaurant?"

"Of course. We're known for that. This is the restaurant of the stars."

"Well, this dog is a movie star," Pamela said.

"Really?" said the man. "And whom am I looking at? Lassie? Toto? Benji? Rin Tin Tin?"

My mother stepped right up to the man.

"Sir," she said, "you are looking at Genghis Khan, the hottest movie star in Hollywood. That's who!"

The man looked at Duz again. Then he smiled.

"Well, of course. I should have known. Who else has such an ugly, mean—"

"You can skip the compliments, pal,"

Pamela said. "We want to eat."

"Come right in," the man said. "Table or booth?"

"Booth," I said. "Duz can jump up and snuggle in."

People looked at us as we walked to our booth.

They were making faces.

Somebody said, "What do you think this is...a *kennel?*"

A little kid was staring at us.

"Genghie!" he shouted. "It's Genghie Khanie!"

"What's a Genghie Khanie?" the lady in the next booth asked.

"He means GENGHIS KHAN!" a man said. "It's the movie star!"

Suddenly people were rushing toward us. "Autographs!" they shouted. "Pawprints!"

"Fur!"

"Pats!"

"Drool!"

"Fleas!"

Everyone wanted something.

"Food!" my father said. "We came here for food."

Pamela got up. "Everybody stand in a neat line. I will hand out numbers. When I call your number, you may come over and gently pat our star. Do not pluck any fur. If a stray hair sticks to your hand, you may keep it."

I stared at Pamela. She was *born* for this Hollywood thing!

The line of people snaked around the room. New people kept coming into the restaurant. The line got longer.

Three hours went by. And we still hadn't ordered our food.

Suddenly a lady shouted, "Forget the fur, the pats, the fleas, whatever! We want to see *The Look!*"

The crowd began chanting:

"We want The Look!

We want The Look!"

Pamela nudged me. "Big trouble," she said.

It was. The crowd wanted to see Duz's famous look of longing. But Duz needed to see or sniff baloney for that look to come on his face.

And it was a secret. His acting coach Ms. Muddlewolf didn't want the public to know about the baloney.

A waiter walked by our table. I saw something on his tray. It was cut up fancy and it had little radishes and green leaves around it. Fancy or not, I knew what it was.

Baloney!

"Stop!" I said to the waiter.

The waiter stopped.

Duz's face got all soft and dreamy and quivery.

The Look.

People applauded.

I grabbed a piece of baloney. But how could I give it to Duz in private?

No problem. Suddenly everyone turned and rushed off to another table.

"Ah, peace!" my father said.

"Ah, Billy Brat," Pamela said.

"Oh no," I said.

Billy Brat was a child star. And the meanest actor in Hollywood! He had just walked in and sat down. Now the crowd was after *him*.

"Does this mean he's more popular than our Duz?" my mother asked.

"Well, his new movie is making tons of money," Pamela said.

Billy Brat looked at us from across the room. He made a nasty face.

Pamela slowly raised her nose and her eyebrows. She glared at Billy. It was a nasty look, but Hollywood style. Where did she learn this stuff!

"Hey, a face-off between you and Billy," I said. "And you just won."

My father stood up. "This is our chance to get out of here," he said.

"It's midnight, and none of us have had anything to eat."

"Except Duz." I laughed.

We drove to a pizza parlor. Duz stayed in the car.

We took the pizza home.

We dragged ourselves into the house.

We gulped down the pizza.

Duz had his with baloney topping. When he finished, he rested his head on my lap.

"Now we can relax," my father said. "A full stomach and no crowds."

He took off his shoes.

"Yes, now we can be normal," my mother said. "No fans, no fur plucking, no Billy Brat."

Pamela yawned. "We can even have a good night's sleep."

They were all wrong.

I found that out four hours later.

3

My mother and father and Pamela went to bed. I was too tired to go to bed. I know that sounds silly. But that's the way it was.

I stretched out on the couch.

Duz put his head on my stomach. He was half asleep and half looking for more baloney. Dogs have a way of doing two things at the same time.

I fell asleep.

I heard a telephone ringing.

Maybe it was ringing in my dreams.

I opened my eyes.

What time was it anyway?

I looked at the clock.

Five A.M.

The telephone was still ringing.

Our telephone number was private. Wrong number, I thought.

I picked up the receiver.

"Quick! Quick!" a voice said.

It was Zero Fogg, Duz's agent.

"Quick, quick, what?" I asked.

"Do you have today's newspaper?"

"It's probably outside," I said.

"Go get it. I'll wait."

"Okay, okay."

I went outside, got the newspaper, and came back. I was still half asleep.

"Got it," I said into the receiver.

"Open it," Zero commanded. "Turn to

page 2. 'Holly's Hollywood.' The show biz column. Read it. I'll wait."

I opened the newspaper. I turned to page 2. There it was—"Holly's Hollywood."

I started reading.

> Our next Academy Award winner? I predict that Duz Shedd, world famous for his canine role in *Genghis Khan: The Challenge,* will win next year's Academy Award as best actor. Move over, Mel and Clint. Make room for the biggest star of them all, Duz Shedd. Duz, make room for your Oscar!

I couldn't believe it. Duz had made only one movie and he was already a Hollywood great.

Now I was *really* awake.

"Oscar! I can just see Duz licking that

little gold statue!" I said.

"I see I have your attention," Zero said. "But there is work to be done. Much, much work."

"Work? Poor Duz needs some time off. He wants to be a regular dog for a while. Last night he got pushed and plucked and pawed. He just wants to snuggle and sniff and fetch and…"

"Listen, he hasn't been *nominated* for best actor yet."

"So?"

"So? We have to make it happen," Zero said. "We need television, newspapers, interviews. Duz's face has to be everywhere."

"But Duz is famous already," I said.

"There is never enough fame," Zero said. "Fame is like eating peanuts. You keep wanting more. You keep needing more."

"Well, if you say so," I said.

"I have to hang up and get to work," Zero said.

"At this hour?" I asked.

"A good agent never sleeps," Zero answered, and he hung up.

My parents shuffled into the room. Boy, did they look tired. Pamela walked in with them.

"Why were you talking on the phone at five o'clock in the morning?" my father grumbled.

"Zero called," I said.

"That would have been my first guess," Pamela said.

"He told me to go out and get the paper."

"Why?" my father asked.

I handed the newspaper to him. I pointed to "Holly's Hollywood." He read it and passed it to my mother. She read it and passed it to Pamela. She read it and passed it to Duz. He sniffed it.

He raised an ear.

The rest of us screamed, "OSCAR!"

And then the phone rang again.

Pamela grabbed the receiver.

"Pamela Brinkman for Duz Shedd," she answered.

Then she was quiet. She was listening. She started to write things down.

"Ten o'clock, noon, two o'clock, four-thirty, gotcha."

She hung up.

"That was Zero," she said. "With Duz's schedule for tomorrow."

"What? I just spoke to him," I said.

Pamela bent down to Duz.

"Lick that fur, wag that tail, show those fangs. You're running for an Oscar nomination!"

Weeks went by.

Duz was showing up all over Hollywood. At parties. At sports events. On TV. In newspapers.

I think he enjoyed it.

Every time he heard the word Oscar, he began to wiggle. Duz wasn't ordinarily a wiggler.

And then one day...the news!

Zero phoned and told us.

Duz Shedd had been nominated for best actor!

YES!

Zero rushed over to our house.

He hugged all of us. Then he said, "You know that Duz is one of five nominees."

"Who are the other four?" Pamela asked.

Zero plopped into a chair. "First, Sir John Richardson. He's been nominated fifteen times. Never won."

"Fifteen times?" my father gasped.

"He's very old," Zero said.

"Next Rugby Polo. He grunts a lot."

"What's that got to do with acting?" my mother asked.

"Grunting can be a high form of acting," Zero said.

"Next. Kip Lancewood. He keeps playing western heroes. People think of *him* as a hero."

"And what's *that* got to do with acting?" my mother asked.

"Nobody's sure. But you gotta respect heroes. You gotta pay attention."

Zero leaned back in his chair. "So what have we got here? A fifteen-time loser, a grunter, and a guy who spends his whole life under a cowboy hat."

"You only told us three names," Pamela said.

Zero snorted. "The fourth is the brat known as Billy Brat."

"What?" I said. "We were in a restaurant and people rushed *away* from Duz and over to *him.*"

"He plays a brat in all his movies," Zero said.

"He's a *real* brat," Pamela said. "He's not acting."

"Exactly," Zero said. "He simply plays himself on the screen. But very few people know that."

"Speaking of people, how many are voting?" my father asked.

"Four thousand eight hundred," Zero said. "We have to keep the publicity going for Duz. The awards will be presented in six weeks."

"So we just keep doing what we've been doing. A snap," I said.

"Well, speaking of snap, we have a small problem," Zero said. "It's picture-snapping time. All the nominees for best actor have been asked to pose together. For the cover of *Glitzy Guys* magazine."

"What's wrong with that?" Pamela asked.

"Duz is the only one with four feet and a tail."

"Well, naturally," my mother said. "If the other actors were dogs, they'd look that way too."

"Speaking of look, what if Duz is asked to do The Look for the picture?" I said. "Where can we hide the baloney?"

Zero stood up. "I'm a top agent," he said. "I make deals, I do lunch, I dream and I scheme. But I do not hide cold cuts. Shedds, you solve the baloney problem."

We were sitting in a small room. Huge photos of *Glitzy Guys* magazine covers were all over the walls. My mother and father and Pamela and I kept stretching our necks to look at them all.

Duz sat quietly in his Genghis Khan costume. Black leather. Blue satin. Goggles. Boots.

"You look terrific, Duz," I said.

Duz wagged his tail.

My mother looked at her watch.

"Where are the others?" she asked.

"They'll come," I said. "Zero said they

would all come to get their pictures taken for a magazine cover."

We were waiting for the other nominees.

"If they don't come, Duz can have the cover all to himself," Pamela said.

"No he can't," a voice said.

A man was looming over us.

"I'm Rugby Polo," he announced.

He bent down to pat Duz. "Loved your movie," he said.

Rugby saluted Duz and went to the refreshments table.

"He didn't grunt at all," Pamela said.

"Hey, look," I said. An old man was coming our way. "It's Sir John."

Sir John Richardson walked up to us and bowed slightly. "Ah, the Shedds," he said. "It is a pleasure to meet you."

"I'm not a real Shedd," Pamela said.

"Just sort of an honorary one."

Sir John stroked Duz. "You are a splendid canine and a superb actor."

Sir John bowed again and walked away.

"Boy, everybody is so nice," I said. "Here comes cowboy Kip."

"Howdy, folks," Kip said. Then he knelt down and rubbed Duz under his snout. "Howdy, pardner. Loved your movie."

Kip tipped his cowboy hat and walked away.

"The other nominees are really friendly," my mother said.

"Here comes Billy Brat," Pamela said.

Billy Brat strutted up to us. He sniffed Duz.

"Yo, mutt," he said. "Is this some kind of joke, putting Mr. Four-legs-and-a-tail in the Oscar race?"

"Now wait a minute," I said. "My dog

is a fine actor and you're being nasty."

"Is Brat your real name?" Pamela asked. "It's so *you*."

"Sure."

I knew it wasn't. Zero had told me it was Klutzabrat.

"So long, loser," Billy said to Duz, and he walked away.

"What a jerk!" Pamela muttered.

Now all the actors were in the room, waiting. Rugby, Sir John, and Kip were drinking coffee and eating pastry. Billy was munching on cookies.

There were no dog bones. I didn't like that.

"Duz is truly the underdog," my mother said.

At last a woman came along and led all of us into a big room. There were cameras and lights and lots of people there.

"Now all you nominees please stand together," the woman said. "While I figure out who goes next to whom."

"Go, Duz," I said.

Duz walked up to the other actors. I hoped that he wouldn't have to stand beside Billy Brat.

The woman angled her head. Back and forth.

Then she said, "Sir John Richardson will be on the very left. Next to him will be Duz Shedd."

Pamela nudged me. "Great! I like Sir John."

Duz walked up to Sir John and licked his fingers. They probably had bits of pastry on them.

"Next, Billy Brat," the woman said.

"Oh no," I gasped.

"It's only for the photo," my father whispered. "It's not a lifelong arrangement."

Billy walked up and stood beside Duz. He sort of snickered at Duz.

"Next, Kip Lancewood, and then, of course, Rugby Polo," the woman said.

Then the woman started to pose the actors. Telling them to stand this way and that way. Get a little closer, get farther apart.

"Make that camera love you," she said.

Duz stood there like all the others. I was so proud of him.

I whispered to Pamela. "I'm glad she didn't ask Duz for The Look."

"Yeah, I was holding my breath," Pamela said.

"Okay, ready to shoot," the woman said.

Suddenly, I saw Billy Brat lift his foot and kick Duz!

Duz looked at Billy. He bared his teeth. Then I heard a terrible growl.

"GRRRRRRRRRRRRRRRRRRRrrrr!!"

Duz sank his teeth into Billy's pants.

R-i-p! Billy Brat's pants started to come down.

The cameras started to snap.

"Great action picture," the woman said.

Sir John said, "This poor dog was kicked."

"Sure was," I said.

My mother and my father and Pamela nodded.

But nobody paid any attention to us.

The woman said, "The camera never lies. I got a picture of this dog biting Billy."

Pamela whispered. "If this gets on a magazine cover, it could ruin Duz's career. It will look like he's attacking his rival for the Oscar."

Billy's pants came all the way down. He was wearing boxer shorts. The word BRAT was printed all over them in gold.

I covered my eyes.

We took Duz to the vet's to make sure he wasn't hurt. He was okay.

But the magazine cover wasn't.

It was awful. There was Duz, with his teeth in Billy's pants! Sir John was looking at Duz. Rugby and Kip were looking straight ahead, as if nothing was happening. Billy's mouth was wide open, as if he was going to faint—or scream.

Things got worse.

There were headlines in all of the newspapers:

BILLY BRAT'S BUTT BITTEN BY MUTT
WILL DUZ DO ANYTHING TO WIN
AN OSCAR?
DUZ SHEDD CHEWS UP THE COMPETITION
DUZ IN THE DOGHOUSE

"These are all lies!" I said. "Duz didn't bite Billy. He only bit his pants. And that's because Billy kicked him."

"There were lots of people there. Why don't they tell the truth?" my father said.

"They work for *Glitzy Guys,*" Pamela said. "And the truth doesn't sell magazines."

"Sir John told the newspapers the truth," my mother said. "But they just say he's old and his eyesight is bad."

"Rugby and Kip should help Duz," Pamela said. "They saw Billy kick Duz. Then they looked away fast."

"Yes, but they won't help," my mother said. "I guess they want Duz out of the Oscar race. And they seemed so nice."

"Uh-oh. Here's another headline," I said.

I held up the newspaper.

BILLY BRAT VOWS TO SUE THE PANTS OFF DUZ SHEDD!

"And hey, here's a picture of Billy's mom. Mrs. Brat. I guess she changed her name too."

"She looks just like Billy," Pamela said.

"Let's try to cheer up," my mother said. "Let's go have lunch at La Roillangelique. Let *the public* see Duz. Let them love him, pat him, worship him again."

"Great idea," I said.

We were off!

When we got there, the same man was at

the door again. I was glad to see him. He knew who we were. He knew our star.

"Hi there," Pamela said. "I guess this time we need no introduction. You remember us?"

"I certainly do," said the man.

Then he looked straight at Duz. "Please LEAVE!!"

"What?" my father said.

"You heard me. We do not accept *vicious* customers. We do not accept customers who might eat other customers instead of the food."

"My dog is gentle..." I began.

Duz wagged his tail.

Pamela gave the man her nasty Hollywood look.

"Someday you'll *beg* us to come back, sir. You'll grovel and whine, but it won't do you any good."

We turned and walked away. We went home.

Nobody was hungry anymore.

Duz walked from room to room with his tail drooping.

"Poor Duz," my father said. "He knows that something is wrong."

"Just remember, Duz didn't do anything wrong," Pamela said. "And besides, Zero and Mr. Swaggs are on our side. They'll figure something out."

Mr. Swaggs was the producer who made Duz's movie. He was an important man in Hollywood.

The next day, Zero and Mr. Swaggs came over to our house. Mr. Swaggs kept muttering the words "damage control."

"How are we controlling this damage?"

my mother asked. We were all having brunch on one of our patios.

My father spoke up. "It's been over a week since that horrible magazine was published. Shouldn't we be giving interviews to defend Duz?"

"That could fuel the flames," Zero said. "Make things worse. We have to lie low and let it all blow over. What's hot news today can be gone tomorrow."

"We hope," Pamela said.

But time went by and nothing blew over. Billy Brat and his parents got themselves on almost every TV show ever invented. They lied their way through all of them.

Zero spent more and more time at our house.

"Billy Brat will get the sympathy vote,"

he said. "It could win him the Oscar."

"I thought the Oscar goes to the best actor," my mother said.

"Yeah, right," Zero said.

I began reading "Holly's Hollywood." Holly was a big fan of Duz's. Maybe I would read something *good* about him.

Nothing.

Then one day, there it was. An item about Duz.

> Update! Some time ago I predicted that Duz Shedd would win the Oscar for best actor. Alas, I must now eat my words. Just like Duz Shedd tried to eat Billy Brat. That carnivorous canine will *never* win the Oscar. Watch Billy Brat take home the prize.

Zero was now sleeping at our house.

"We have to do something," I whispered to Pamela one morning. "Zero's blow-over isn't working."

Pamela and I talked and talked. Do this. Do that. No. Yes. No. Maybe.

Duz stretched out at our feet and listened.

At last I said, "Agreed?"

And Pamela answered, "Agreed."

Zero woke up. We waited until he had his five cups of coffee.

Then I said, "We want to put Duz on *Tippy's Trashtalk* TV show."

"*What?* Even Billy Brat didn't go on that one."

"He doesn't have to," I said. "We do."

"Maybe this show can save Duz," Pamela said. "Remember DumpWump, the TV clown. His career was at rock bottom before he went on that show. Now he's a star again."

"But more careers are ruined than saved on that show," Zero said. "Tippy is awful. Her motto is 'Trash is cash.'"

"We're desperate," I said. "Can you get Duz on?"

"No problem," Zero said. "Tippy loves the desperate, the demolished, the disgraced."

Pamela and I looked at each other. Were we *crazy?*

7

Duz and I were on a stage in a TV studio. We were sitting on big, soft, cushy chairs. There were empty chairs on either side of us.

There was a big studio audience in front of us.

My parents and Pamela and Zero were watching in the wings.

Tippy introduced Duz and me.

"Folks, I want you to meet the hottest dog star in the world today. Duz Shedd, otherwise known as Genghis Khan.

"And with him is his owner, Fred Shedd.

"Duz and Fred have agreed to come on my show to give us their exclusive version of the Billy Brat dog-bite incident."

I stood up. "It was a dog-*kick* incident. Billy kicked my dog."

The audience mumbled.

Tippy smiled. But her teeth were clenched.

"We'll hear from you in just a bit, Fred. But first I want to introduce my other distinguished guest. The pet psychologist known far and wide as Dr. Canine. Dr. Canine's latest book is *Why Good Dogs Go Bad.*"

Duz growled.

A man walked onto the stage, bowed, and sat down beside me.

Tippy turned to me. "Now, Fred, here's your chance to tell your story."

"It's not a story, it's the truth," I said. "Billy kicked Duz for no reason. But Duz didn't bite Billy. He just pulled down Billy's pants. Duz is a whole bunch nicer than Billy."

Duz raised an ear. I patted him.

Tippy turned to Dr. Canine. "Doctor?"

Dr. Canine leaned forward. "As my book points out, good dogs *do* go bad," he said.

I turned to Dr. Canine. "My dog didn't go bad. You're just trying to sell your book!"

Tippy looked happy. She loved fights on her program. She didn't care who won. She didn't care who was right.

"Boooooooooo!"

The audience was booing.

Were they booing me or Dr. Canine?

Me!

Dr. Canine kept on talking. The audience applauded.

I slouched in my chair while he went on and on.

"What makes a good dog go bad?" he said. "Bad kibble. Bad bones. Bad flea powder. Bad toys. Bad owners. Bad..."

Pamela and I had made a terrible mistake! Duz and I should never have come on this program. His career was probably over.

But Duz seemed relaxed. He fell asleep while Dr. Canine was saying that even a bad haircut could make a dog go bad.

I wished *I* could fall asleep until the show was over. But I had to sit and listen to Dr. Canine.

Suddenly Tippy cut him short. She said it was time to bring on another guest.

"Folks, I have a wonderful surprise for you today. Let's say hello to Billy Brat! Yes! Billy Brat...actor, victim...has agreed to come on my show. And for the first time since the incident, he will face his attacker!"

The audience exploded in cheers.

This was awful!

Duz started to sniff in his sleep.

Suddenly he woke up.

Billy Brat limped onto the stage. He was wearing short pants. I could see a long red scar on his leg!

He limped into the chair farthest from Duz.

Tippy bent down to him.

"Now, Billy, I see that you still have a wound from Duz's attack. The camera will close in on it, if you don't mind."

"Just don't touch it," Billy said. "It hurts so much."

Duz sat up straight. He was still sniffing. His nose started to twitch.

Suddenly he leaped across the stage toward Billy. He had learned that leap for his movie. It was fast, strong, and SCARY.

I couldn't stop him. Nobody could. He

was now the mighty Genghis Khan.

He stopped in front of Billy Brat. He opened his mouth. He leaned toward Billy's leg…

I wanted to close my eyes but I couldn't.

Duz's mouth was on Billy's leg.

Tippy was so happy she couldn't stand it.

"Folks, another attack by this monster dog," she said. "And you see it here...on my show!"

All eyes were on Duz. The cameras were on Duz. And there he was, *licking* the top of Billy's leg.

Duz licked the leg clean! The red scar was gone.

I ran over to Duz. Now *I* was sniffing. Sniffing Duz.

Duz had some red stuff smeared around his mouth.

"Billy Brat's wound was made of KETCHUP!" I said. "It's fake, just like I told you!"

The whole audience seemed to gasp at one time.

Tippy looked disappointed. But it didn't last long.

"A fake!" she said. "And you found out on *my* show. Billy Brat has been lying. Poor Duz, he's truly a lovely pooch."

"And a fine actor," I said. "Did you see that Genghis leap?"

My parents, Pamela, and Zero came rushing out to the stage. We all hugged.

Duz was busy licking ketchup off the side of his mouth.

8

Duz's career was saved. And he had done it himself. The ketchup story went all over the world.

DUZ FINALLY LICKS BRAT!
KETCHUP-GATE!
BILLY BRAT'S COVER-UP EXPOSED

There was a special "Holly's Hollywood" column. It began: "How do you say 'I'm sorry' to a dog?"

Holly wrote that Duz was gentle, smart, talented, and would win the Oscar.

Duz got presents from strangers.

Mostly ketchup. All brands. All sizes.

Zero sent flowers.

Mr. Swaggs sent engraved dog bowls.

Ms. Muddlewolf sent us cartons of baloney.

That was Duz's favorite present.

"Baloney!" Pamela said. "If we could only figure out how to keep some of this handy. Just in case Duz is asked for The Look again."

"But how?" I said. "If we bring baloney out for Duz, everybody will see it."

"That's it!" Pamela said. "Let everybody see it."

Pamela grabbed a slice of baloney. She rolled it up. Very, very tightly.

Then she held it up like a pen.

It looked like a reddish, pinkish pen.

Pamela took a piece of paper out of her pocket.

She walked over to Duz.

She stuck the paper and rolled-up slice of baloney in his face.

"May I have your autograph?" she asked.

The Look spread across Duz's face!

"Perfect!" I said.

Zero walked into the room. "Are you ready for the Academy Awards? The big Oscar night?"

Duz wiggled.

"Sure," I said. "I can see it now. Somebody says, 'The envelope, please.' She opens the envelope. Takes out a paper. Reads the name on the paper. 'The winner is...Duz Shedd!'"

"You can't be sure," Zero said.

"Well, this is how I figure it," I said. "Kip and Rugby never spoke up for Duz. So they're not so popular anymore. And you don't think that Billy Brat..."

"That dog-kicker?" Zero said. "He can't win. He'll be lucky if he ever makes another movie."

"So that just leaves Sir John," Pamela said. "And he *always* loses."

"So far," Zero said. "So far."

I wished he hadn't said that.

9

It's Oscar night. Hollywood's biggest night.

Fritz drove us here in the limo.

I'm outside the auditorium with Duz, my parents, and Pamela.

We're going to make an entrance.

On the red carpet.

Everybody is in their best clothes. I'm in a tuxedo. So is Duz.

Ready…set…now! Cameras click, flashbulbs flash. We sort of sweep through the crowd. People are screaming and reaching out. They want to touch Duz.

Duz raises an ear, and the crowd goes crazy.

Now we're inside and sitting down. Duz is next to me, then Pamela, my parents, Zero, Mr. Swaggs, Ms. Muddlewolf, and other people from the studio.

Sir John Richardson is sitting on the other side of me. Sir John and I have become good friends. He's so nice that I kind of want *him* to win the Oscar. But I want my dog to win too. And they can't both win.

The ceremony starts. Winners are announced. Best this, best that. People go up onto the stage to get their Oscars. There's dancing. And speeches. And singing. And dancing. And more awards and more singing and dancing and speeches.

Duz wiggles every time he hears the word Oscar.

It seems as if they'll never get around to Best Actor.

I look at my watch. We've been sitting here over two hours.

At last Zara Zeeker comes on the stage. She's the actress who's going to announce Best Actor.

I lean over and whisper to Sir John, "Good luck."

"Oh, I certainly hope not," he whispers back. "If I win, I'll probably never get nominated again. I love nominations."

He didn't *want* to win!

I look back up to the stage. Zara Zeeker is telling a few jokes.

Then she gets serious. She says, "Nominees for the best actor in a leading role are…"

I shiver all over when she comes to

"Duz Shedd in *Genghis Khan: The Challenge.*"

Then they show a clip of Duz in the movie. There he is, on the big screen.

At last all the nominees are announced.

Zara says, "The envelope, please."

A lady appears and hands Zara an envelope.

Zara opens it and takes out a paper.

She reads the name on the paper. "And the Oscar goes to...*Duz Shedd!!!*"

She yells it loud and clear.

Duz hears his name called. He leaps out of his seat, scrambles over me and Sir John, and runs up onto the stage.

I run after him.

Everybody starts to laugh.

We're at the mike. Zara hands the Oscar to Duz.

He opens his mouth.

It's not a good fit.

"I'll take it," I say.

The Oscar feels terrific in my hands.

The audience is waiting for a speech.

Duz raises an ear.

The audience claps.

"Let's see his famous Look!" a voice cries out.

It's Billy Brat. Does he know our secret?

Duz just stands there with his raised ear.

"C'mon," Billy yells. "Show us The Look, Mr. Great Actor!"

Billy Brat is trying to spoil Duz's big moment.

"Autograph!" someone shouts.

It's Pamela. She's running toward the stage. She's holding her baloney pen and a piece of paper.

We're saved!

"STOP!!" An usher yells at Pamela. Then he stands in her way.

She's stuck.

Now the auditorium is quiet. So quiet.

Everyone is waiting for Duz and The Look.

Duz looks to the left. Then he looks to the right. Then slowly and perfectly the dreamy soft Look spreads across his face.

He did it himself! Without baloney!

He really is a great actor!

The audience goes wild. They stand up and applaud and applaud.

Pamela slips around the usher. She dashes up to the stage. She hands the pen to Duz.

"You deserve a reward," she whispers.

Duz gulps down the baloney pen.

The audience goes wild again.

They think the mighty Genghis ate a metal pen!

I raise the Oscar high.

"Duz Shedd thanks you for this Oscar and says he will never eat it."

Then Duz, Pamela, and I leave the stage.

I feel so proud.

Suddenly Duz pokes his nose into Pamela's pocket. He's walking and poking at the same time.

Pamela has a pocketful of baloney pens.

I hope nobody notices.

Don't miss the next Genghis Khan book!

Suddenly, Babs was on the floor, staring at Duz.

"My, you really are ugly-looking, aren't you?" she said.

"Extremely," my father said proudly.

Babs was still eyeballing Duz.

"Duz, could you show us how you live? Could you give us a tour of your dog house?"

Duz wagged his tail. He ran to his bedroom. He leaped onto his bed.

"A bone-shaped bed!" Babs said. "I should have known."

From *Genghis Khan: Interview with the Dog Star* by Marjorie Weinman Sharmat

Don't miss the *second* Genghis Khan book!

"My name is Fritz," the man said. "I have a limo for you."

We settled back in a beautiful silver car. "My first limo," my mother sighed.

We drove through neighborhoods with huge homes and big trees. At last we stopped in front of a house that looked like it belonged to a…well…a movie star!

There were three acres. And palm trees. And a swimming pool. Awesome!

"This is ours?" my father said.

"Your home sweet home for a year," Fritz told us.

From *Genghis Khan: A Dog Star Is Born* by Marjorie Weinman Sharmat

MARJORIE WEINMAN SHARMAT is best known for creating super-sleuth Nate the Great. Her books have been translated into fourteen languages and have won numerous awards. She insists that Duz is not based on her dog, Dudley—who, she says, is "definitely cute" and has never won an Oscar.

Ms. Sharmat lives with her husband, Mitchell. They have two sons—Craig and Andrew—and a grandson, Nathan.